A First-Start Easy Reader

This easy reader contains only 41 different words,
repeated often to help the young reader develop
word recognition and interest in reading.

Basic word list for *Skating on Thin Ice*

all	help	slow
always	is	slower
and	it	smiles
any	Joe	sometimes
at	likes	than
best	look	they
but	now	to
cries	out	together
dizzy	Rosie	too
fast	saves	twirls
faster	she	way
Flo	skate	when
getting	skates	whirls
he		with

Skating on Thin Ice

Written by Louise Everett

Illustrated by Richard Max Kolding

Troll Associates

Library of Congress Cataloging in Publication Data

Everett, Louise.
    Skating on thin ice.

    Summary: In this easy-to-read story, Rosie the
elephant and her friend Joe enjoy ice skating
until Joe falls into the ice.
    [1. Ice skating—Fiction.   2. Friendship—
Fiction.   3. Elephants—Fiction]   I. Kolding,
Richard Max, ill.   II. Title.
PZ7.E918Sk   1987   [E]   86-30857
ISBN 0-8167-0992-0 (lib. bdg.)
ISBN 0-8167-0993-9 (pbk.)

Rosie likes to skate.

She likes to skate fast.

She likes to skate slow.

She likes to skate any way at all.

Joe likes to skate, too.

He likes to skate fast.

He likes to skate slow.

He likes to skate any way at all.

Sometimes, Rosie skates
faster than Joe.

Sometimes, Joe skates
faster than Rosie.

Sometimes, Rosie skates
slower than Joe.

Sometimes, Joe skates
slower than Rosie.

Rosie likes it best when
they skate together.

Flo likes to skate, too.

She likes to skate with Joe.

Flo smiles.

Joe smiles.

Flo whirls.

Joe twirls.

Joe whirls.

Joe twirls.

Joe is getting dizzy.

Look out, Joe!

"Help," cries Joe.

"Help," cries Flo.

Rosie saves Joe.

Now, Joe skates fast

and Joe skates slow . . .

but he always skates with Rosie.